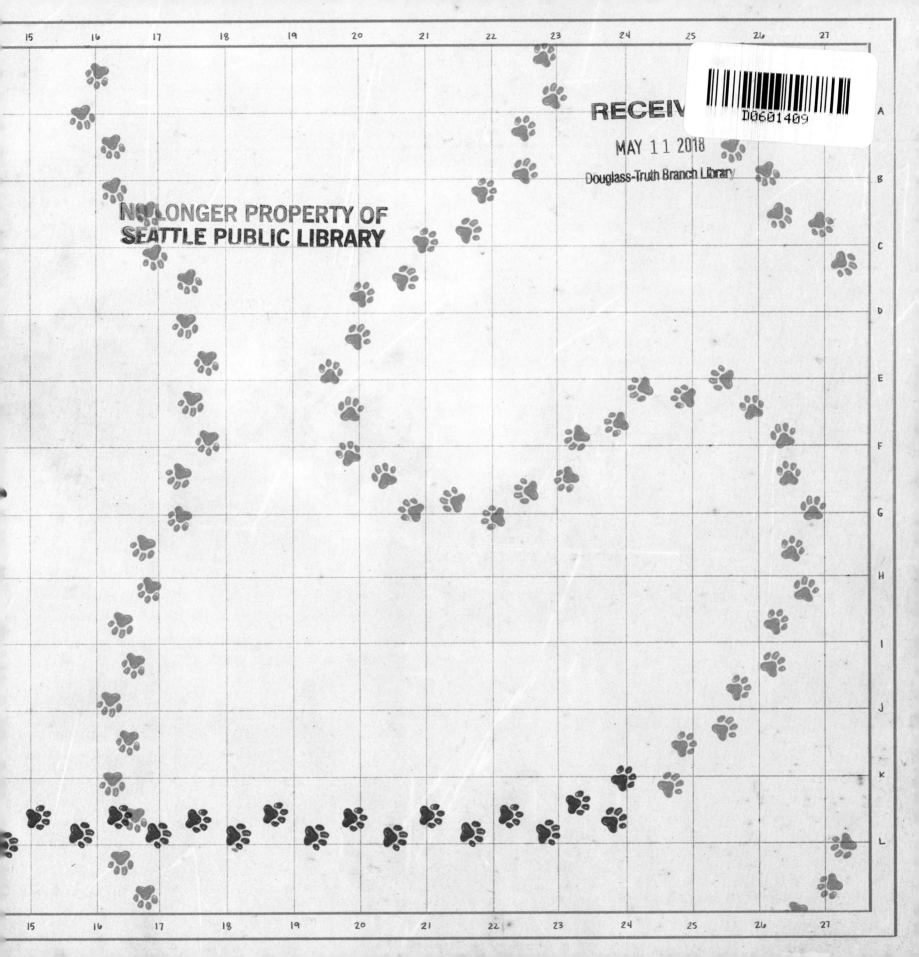

THIS BOOK IS DEDICATED TO TWO LITTLE RASCALS.

TO MY DOG, MIDJI, WHO INSPIRED THE STORY AND

TAUGHT ME ABOUT UNCONDITIONAL LOVE. AND TO MY

DAUGHTER, FRANKIE, WHO SHOWED ME THERE IS NO

LIMIT TO HOW MUCH LOVE A HEART CAN HOLD. -A.B.

STERLING CHILDREN'S BOOKS
New York

An Imprint of Sterling Publishing Co., Inc.
1166 Avenue of the Americas
New York, NY 10036

ISBN 978-1-4549-2678-8

Distributed in Canada by Sterling Publishing Co., Inc.
c/o Canadian Manda Group, 664 Annette Street
Toronto, Ontario M6S 2C8, Canada
Distributed in the United Kingdom by GMC Distribution Services
Castle Place, 166 High Street, Lewes, East Sussex BN7 1XU, England
Distributed in Australia by NewSouth Books
45 Beach Street, Coogee, NSW 2034, Australia

For information about custom editions, special sales, and premium and corporate purchases,
please contact Sterling Special Sales at 800-805-5489 or specialsales@sterlingpublishing.com.

Manufactured in China

Lot #:
2 4 6 8 10 9 7 5 3 1
02/18

sterlingpublishing.com

Cover and interior design by Heather Kelly

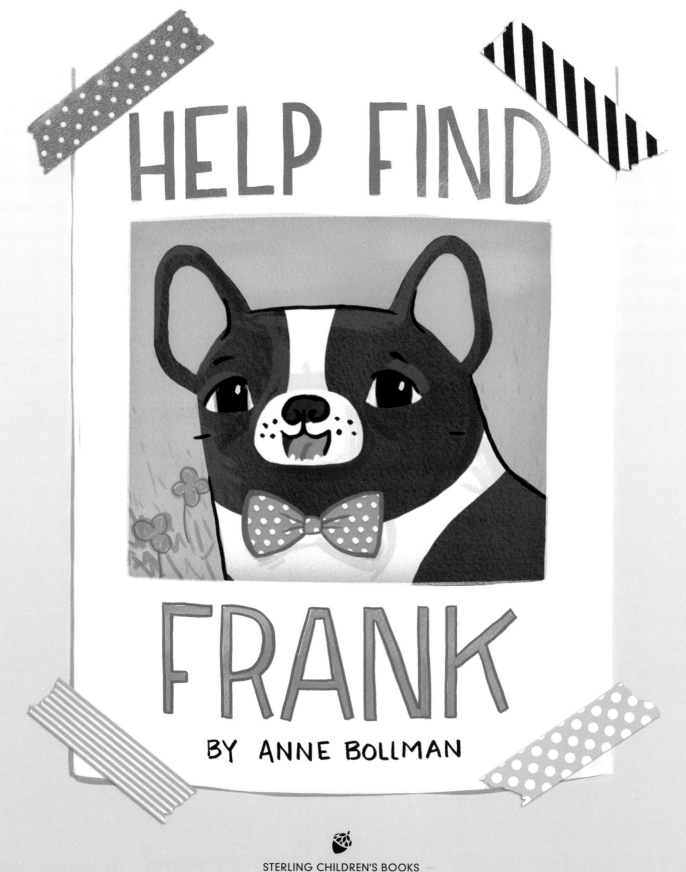

HELP FIND FRANK

BY ANNE BOLLMAN

STERLING CHILDREN'S BOOKS
New York

This is Frank.

Frank is lost.

We should help find him.

There are some things you should know about Frank.

He loves to run and play, but he overheats easily.

EXHIBIT A

Then he finds ways to cool off.

EXHIBIT B

BEWARE his slobbery kisses!

He gives them out regardless of
whether or not anyone wants one.

EXHIBIT C

Frank loves to play fetch,

EXHIBIT D

but he skips the part where he brings the ball back.

EXHIBIT E

Frank has **VERY** stinky toots.

EXHIBIT F

Whatever you do,
DO NOT feed him
any cheese. You've
been warned.

Frank loves everyone—
except the mail carrier.

GRRRRRRr

EXHIBIT G

His favorite animal is a squirrel.
Let's hope he never catches one.

EXHIBIT H

Okay, now that you know a bit
about Frank, let's go find him!

INTERVIEW I: FRANK'S FAMILY

NOTE A: "FRANK WAS LAST SEEN RUNNING DOWN THE STREET IN FRONT OF OUR HOUSE."

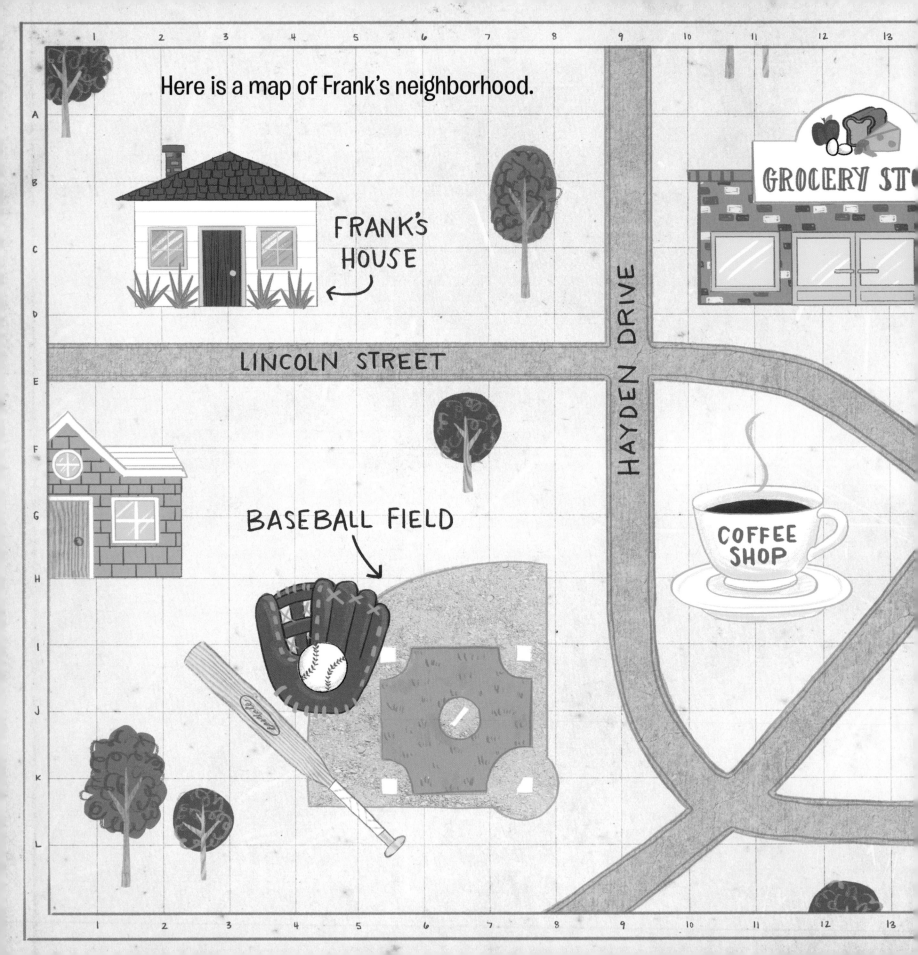

Here is a map of Frank's neighborhood.

FRANK'S HOUSE

GROCERY ST

LINCOLN STREET

HAYDEN DRIVE

BASEBALL FIELD

COFFEE SHOP

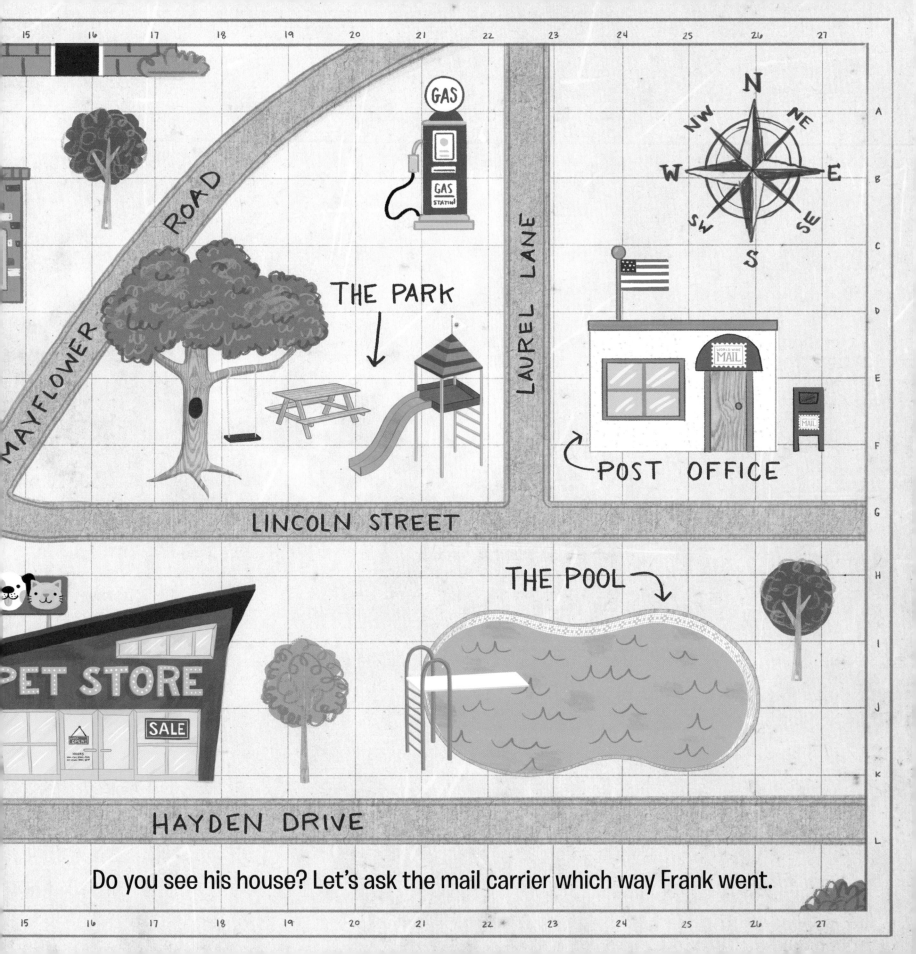

Do you see his house? Let's ask the mail carrier which way Frank went.

INTERVIEW 2: THE MAIL CARRIER

"HE CHASED MY MAIL TRUCK

SOUTHEAST ON LINCOLN STREET."

Where do you think
Frank ended up?

HINT: CHECK EXHIBIT A!

Yes, let's look at the park! **Fraaaaaank!**
Do you see any sign of Frank? What else can you find?

CAN YOU FIND...

PEEKING EYES?
A SNAIL?
A BUTTERFLY?
A BEE?
A TENNIS BALL?
A LOLLIPOP?
A KITE?
A BIRD'S NEST?
A SNAKE?
A JUMP ROPE?
A BASEBALL HAT?
A BUNNY?
A RACCOON?
A TOY TRUCK?
A TRICYCLE?
FRANK'S BOW TIE?

Maybe that girl on the swing will know where he is!

INTERVIEW 3: GIRL ON THE SWING

"HE PLAYED TAG WITH US AND WE SHARED A SNACK WITH HIM. THEN HE SAW A SQUIRREL AND CHASED IT SOUTHWEST DOWN MAYFLOWER ROAD."

Where do you think Frank went next? What else does he like to do?

HINT: REFER TO EXHIBIT D!

MAP

FRANK'S HOUSE

LINCOLN STREET

HAYDEN DRIVE

GROCERY STORE

MAYFLOWER ROAD

THE PARK

GAS

LAUREL LANE

POST OFFICE

LINCOLN STREET

BASEBALL FIELD

COFFEE SHOP

PET STORE
SALE

THE POOL

HAYDEN DRIVE

Yep: fetch balls! You're right—he could be at the baseball field.

Fraaaaaaaaaaaaank!

Are there any clues that Frank was here?

GO BLUE!

CAN YOU FIND...

A GROUNDHOG?
ANTS?
BARE FEET?
MISSING SHOES?
SOMEONE TAKING A PICTURE?
SUNGLASSES?
A BANANA PEEL?
SOMEONE PEEKING?
A BATTING GLOVE?
THE SQUIRREL?
A BABY?
A MOUSE?
A FOAM FAN FINGER?
A PURSE?
PEANUTS?

Let's ask a baseball player if he saw Frank.

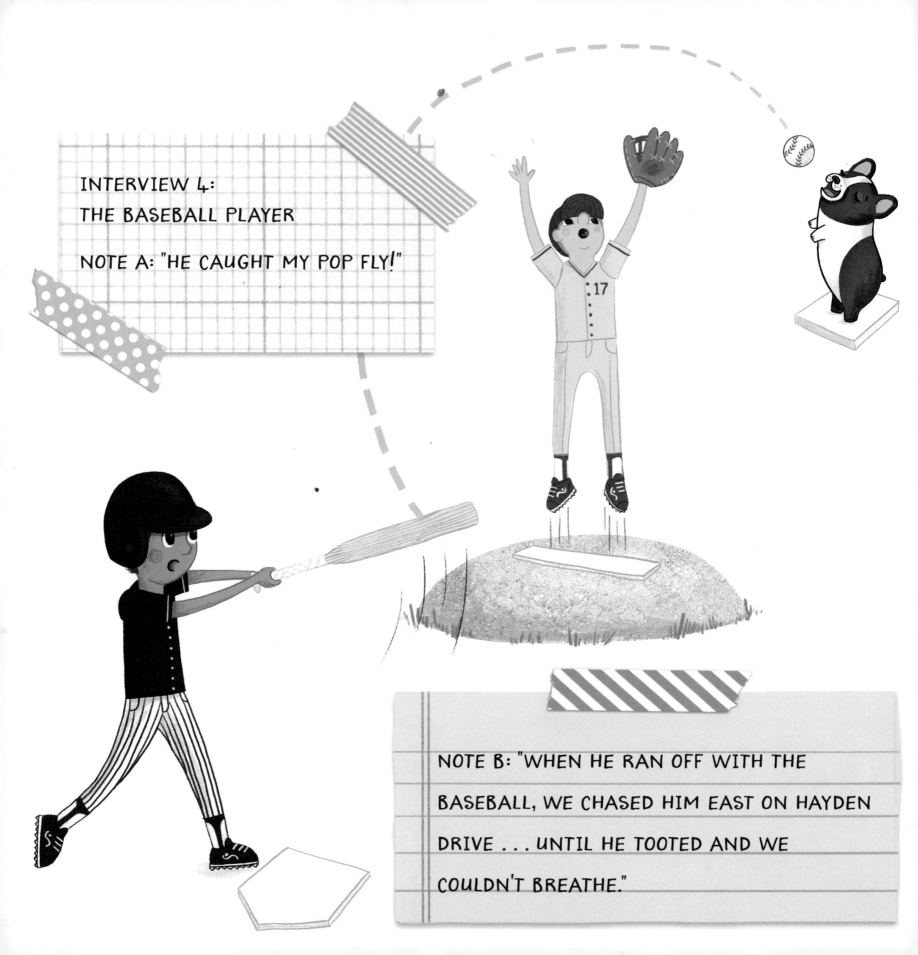

MAP

FRANK'S HOUSE

GROCERY STORE

GAS

THE PARK

LINCOLN STREET

HAYDEN DRIVE

MAYFLOWER ROAD

LAUREL LANE

POST OFFICE

BASEBALL FIELD

COFFEE SHOP

LINCOLN STREET

PET STORE

SALE

THE POOL

HAYDEN DRIVE

Uh-oh, did someone feed him cheese?

Hey! The pet store is east on Hayden Drive. Maybe we should buy him a toy. That way, if we find him, we have a way to get him to come to us.

Pick out a toy for Frank. Which toy do you think he would like? What was his favorite animal again?

HINT: REFER TO EXHIBIT H!

DOG TOYS $5.00 ea.

01572 6003119 8461

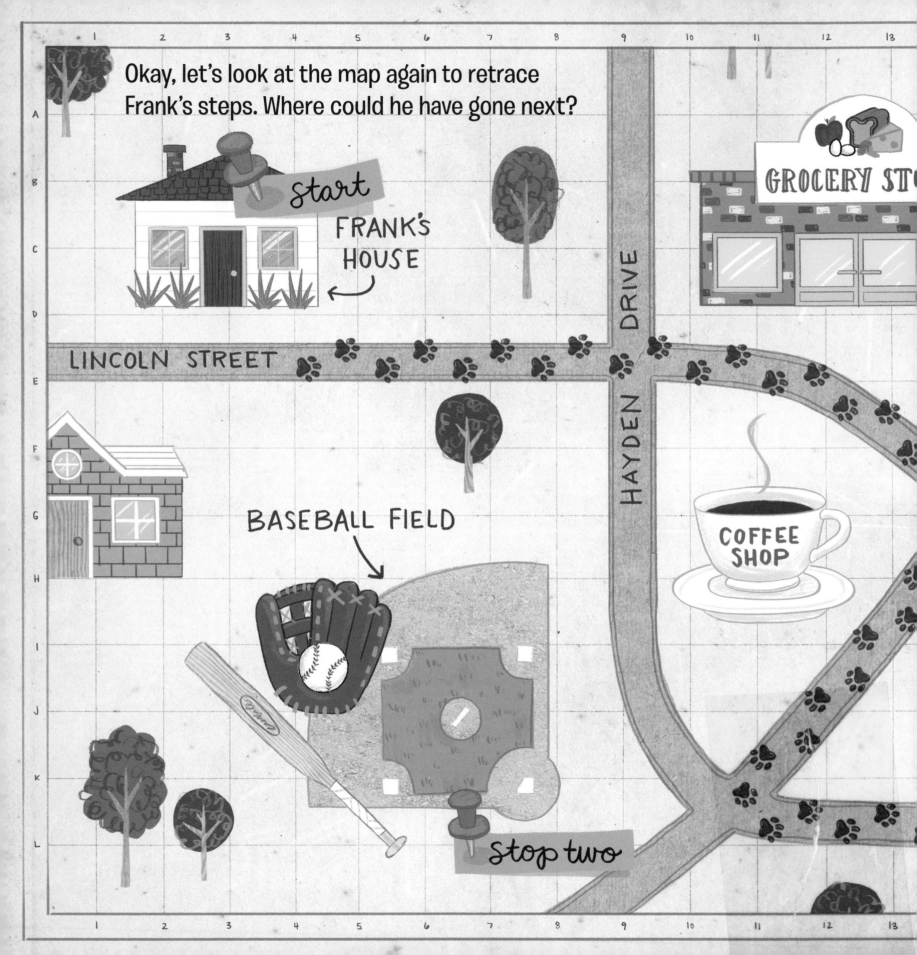

Okay, let's look at the map again to retrace Frank's steps. Where could he have gone next?

Start

FRANK'S HOUSE

GROCERY STO

LINCOLN STREET

HAYDEN DRIVE

BASEBALL FIELD

COFFEE SHOP

Stop two

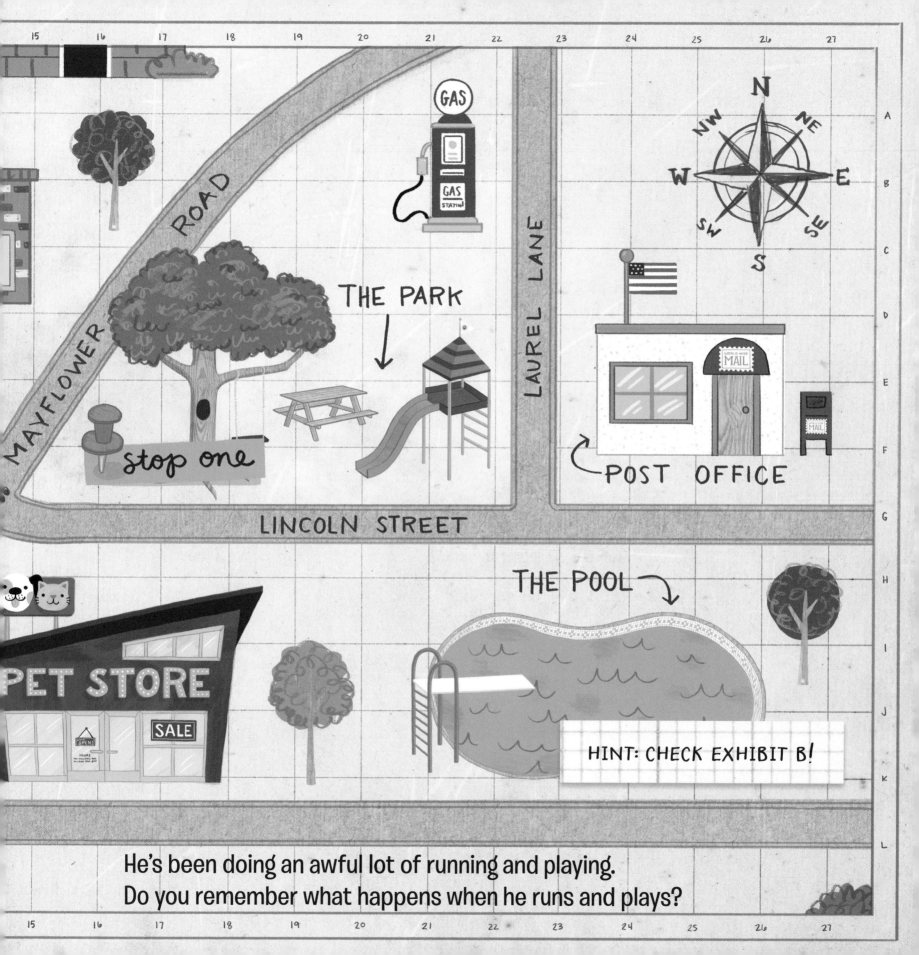

THE PARK

stop one

THE POOL

POST OFFICE

PET STORE
SALE

HINT: CHECK EXHIBIT B!

He's been doing an awful lot of running and playing.
Do you remember what happens when he runs and plays?

CAN YOU FIND...

MELTING ICE CREAM?

A RUBBER DUCKY?

SOMEONE BREAKING A RULE?

A SEAGULL?

SWIMMER'S FLIPPERS?

SUNGLASSES?

DIVING RINGS?

A MOUSE?

A GAME OF CHICKEN?

A FISH?

A NOODLE FIGHT?

A HANDSTAND?

THE LIFEGUARD?

FLIP-FLOPS?

THE STOLEN BASEBALL?

FRANK?!?!

ICE CREAM

$5

SUN BLOCK

YOU FOUND FRANK!!!

Now it's time for your reward . . .

. . . a slobbery kiss!

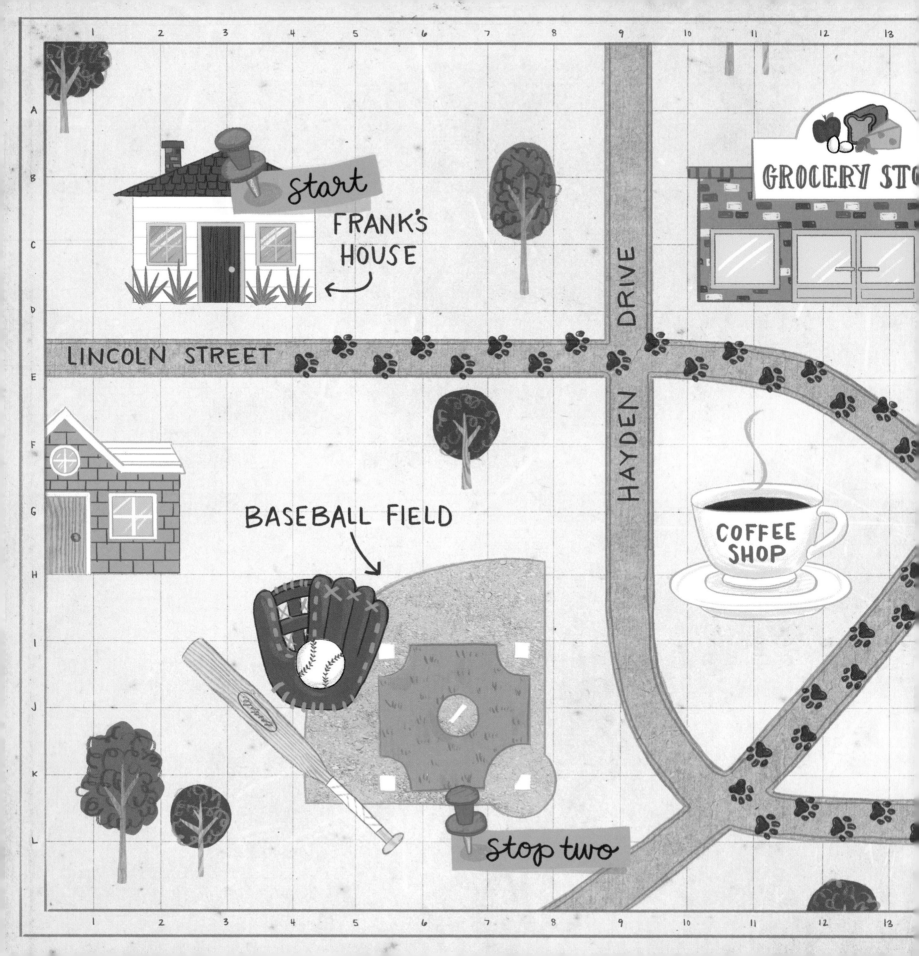